By Amanda Miles

Pictures by N.P.Monaghan

ISBN: 978-1-9999383-0-7

A CIP catalogue record for this book is available from the British
Library

For Paul

Thank you to my family for their continued support and to all the dancers and teachers at the Griffin Lynch Dance school. Without you all there would be no book.

CONTENTS

Chapter 1

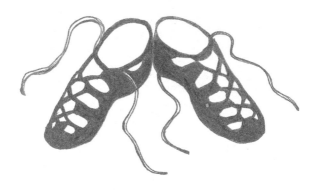

Grace stared at the framed photographs dotted along the wall. She hadn't been tall enough to see them last year but just recently she had 'shot up', so everyone kept telling her.

One photograph caught her attention. It was of a young girl wearing a pretty patterned dress, school socks and ballet pumps. She couldn't see the colour of the dress as the photograph was an old black and white one. The girl was holding a trophy.

"So, what do you feel like doing on the first day of your holidays?" Aunty Mary's brown eyes sparkled mischievously.

Grace looked out of the window at her dad and twin brother, Patrick, playing football in the garden. She felt a little envious if she was honest. They loved football and if they weren't playing it, they were watching matches on the television or talking about the latest results.

They were the best of friends and, although she loved her dad and brother very much, she felt left out as if she didn't belong to their secret club. It hadn't really bothered her before but it did now there was just the three of them.

Grace's eyes started to sparkle like Aunty Mary's and she wiped away a tear that had managed to escape down onto her cheek.

"I think you and I need to get outside but not to play football."

They went to get their coats. It was a gorgeous day with the sun shining but enough frost in the air to let you know it was definitely winter.

Her dad and Patrick stopped playing when they saw Grace and Aunty Mary. "You off?" her father panted, the air escaping his mouth like steam from a kettle.

"We thought we'd go for a walk. Put some colour in our cheeks like you," Aunty Mary answered.

"Have a good time," he said and then the boys carried on with their game.

Grace and Aunty Mary walked down the street. This should have only taken five minutes but it seemed everyone was on the street enjoying the winter sunshine and they all wanted to stop and chat. The conversations were all the same.

"Good morning, Mary. It's a lovely day, isn't it? Did you hear about Jerry over in Ballina? Shocking, isn't it? I shouldn't say anymore in front of this young lady. And who are you? Oh, Kate's daughter. May her soul rest in peace. She's just like her mum too. So sad! So terrible to lose her so young."

It was at this point that Aunty Mary

would make their excuses and they would carry on walking until the next neighbour stopped them.

Her dad had thought it would be good for them to escape London for a while, away from prying questions and endless sympathy but it was just the same here. So many questions and people asking how they felt all the time. How would they feel if their mother had died from cancer six months ago?

At the end of the road was the local high street. Rows of coloured shop buildings, all stuck together. Each building slightly taller than the next as the street rose up towards the clock tower at the end. Fairy lights draped along the top of the shop fronts, lighting up the goods inside.

Grace liked the busyness of the street. She was lost in a huge crowd of people, all out Christmas shopping. Invisible. Just how she liked it.

She was looking at a row of iced cupcakes in the baker's window when she heard some music. Turning around, she saw some shoppers walking up to the clock tower where the music was coming from.

"What's that?" Grace asked her aunt.

"It's the Christmas festival. I'd forgotten it was today. Would you like to watch?"

Grace nodded.

They walked over to the large crowd that

had gathered. Aunty Mary pushed her to the front so she had a better view. There was a small raised stage and in the middle stood three men playing musical instruments; a violin, drum and a black coloured flute. The music they played was lively and the musicians tapped their feet as they moved around the stage. Grace loved it and found herself bouncing up and down in time with the music. Aunty Mary came up behind her.

"This is traditional Irish music. They are playing a fiddle, pipe and bodhran; that's the drum."

The band soon got everyone clapping with them and for the first time, since Grace had arrived in Ireland, she felt really happy.

Chapter 2

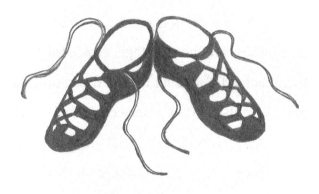

After a few songs the musicians stopped playing and the crowd cheered. Once the clapping had died down, one of the musicians addressed the crowd.

"Thank you everyone and welcome to the Westport Christmas festival. We'd like to introduce a group of girls who have kindly

agreed to dance for us all now. Please welcome
the Cole School of Irish dancing."

Grace watched as eight girls, all dressed
in identical costumes, stepped onto the stage.
Their dresses were gold and green covered in
diamonds that shone in the winter sunlight and
dazzled the audience.

Some of the girls had short hair decorated
with diamond hair bands and some had long hair
with a tumble of curls that spilled down their

backs. It looked to Grace like they were wearing white school socks and shoes that looked like ballet pumps, only they were black not pink.

They stood in a line with a partner and held each other's hand in the air, pointing their right foot forward.

The musicians began to play a lively beat while the girls stood very still. Suddenly they started to move, each pair bouncing up and down lightly on their feet. First their legs were straight, then bent behind them, then crossed over as they moved across the stage. Grace watched as their legs kicked up their skirts. They looked like they were flying.

But their arms were very different. They were either joined to another girl by their hands or down by their sides and very, very still.

'That's strange,' thought Grace. 'Their legs are so free but their arms are like prisoners strapped to their sides.'

Grace watched as the girls danced in and out of each other, always ending up where they had started and always in perfect unison. Finally, the last note was played and the girls stopped with one foot crossed over the other. The crowd cheered as the girls walked off the stage.

Grace turned around to face Aunty Mary. Her aunt saw she was smiling and there was some colour in her cheeks.

"Well, you look happier. Did you enjoy that?"

"That was amazing," gushed Grace. "Their legs moved so fast and they were so elegant and graceful. I've never seen dancing like that before. I mean it's a bit like ballet and tap dancing, but different."

Grace couldn't stop talking. "The way they danced in time to the music and moved around each other. I don't think I could do that. I think I would have crashed into the other dancers. It must have taken them ages to learn to dance like that. But their arms? That was

strange. Why were their arms so still?"

Grace looked at her Aunt who had been waiting for her to take a breath.

"Finally you stop talking," she laughed. "Well, this is Irish dance and the focus is on the feet. As the dances are so quick and the feet have to do such amazing steps, the people who invented the dance, all those years ago, decided they wanted everyone to look just at their legs and not get distracted by what the dancer's arms were doing."

"That makes sense, I suppose."

"Modern dances today," continued her aunt, "sometimes have arm movements but traditional dances like these don't."

Just then the musicians started to play again. As Grace watched them play their instruments, her feet started to move to the music and all she wanted to do was dance. A feeling she'd never had before.

After a couple more songs, Aunty Mary tapped her on her shoulder and beckoned for her to follow. "Sorry, sweetie, but we have to go now."

Grace's smile disappeared. "Are the dancers coming back on stage?"

"No, honey. They were only doing one

dance. Why? Would you like to see more Irish dancing?"

"Yes, please!"

"Okay. Why don't I find out about any local dances going on and I promise I'll take you. How about that?"

Grace's smile returned.

"Thank you," she said. "I'd like that."

"Well, that's sorted. Now, let's go and get some of those cupcakes you were looking at earlier before they all go."

Grace reached out for Aunty Mary's hand and squeezed it tightly. She felt happy and it felt good.

Chapter 3

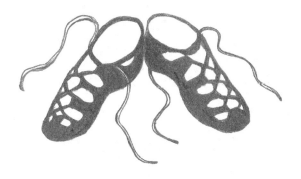

Grace raced around to the back door of Aunty Mary's house and ran inside. Patrick and her dad were sitting on the sofa, eating currant cake, in front of the television.

"Dad, I've just seen some Irish dancing. They were amazing. They moved their feet so quickly and they looked beautiful in these green and gold dresses. And there were musicians playing these funny instruments. Well, they looked like instruments we have back home but different, but anyway Aunty Mary says she's going to take me to see some more Irish dancing. Isn't that brilliant?"

Grace's dad was astounded. He hadn't seen her this animated in ages.

"That's exciting! I didn't know you liked Irish dancing?"

"What's Irish dancing?" said Patrick, looking up from the television.

"It's this amazing type of dancing where your feet move really fast and you kick your legs in the air but you keep your arms still by your side."

"That sounds weird," said Patrick, even more confused with Grace's explanation. "They must move like penguins. They can't move their arms either."

"Oh, shut up, Patrick. You don't know

16

what it's like. You didn't see."

"Well, I don't want to see. It sounds boring!"

"Now, now, you two," said Aunty Mary, bringing in a pot of tea. "Let's not argue." She turned to look at Grace's dad. "Michael, I can't believe you never told the children about Irish dancing."

Michael looked up alarmed, crumbs of cake stuck to the side of his face. "It never came up. River Dance was over years before they were born."

"I'm not talking about River Dance. I mean Irish dancing like Kate used to do."

Grace looked at her dad. "Mum used to do Irish dancing. You never told me."

"As I said, it never came up," said Dad wiping his mouth. "Your mother never talked about it. She thought it was part of her old life."

"That will never do. These children need to know their heritage, where they've come from," said Aunty Mary, shaking her head at Michael who looked like a child who had just been told off.

Aunty Mary left the room and returned with a framed photograph in her hands. She gave it to Grace. It was the one she had been looking at this morning, with the little girl holding a trophy.

"This was your mother when she was

eight. She won her first trophy at that Feis. The light jig, if I remember correctly."

"What's a fish?" asked Grace, giving the photograph to Patrick.

Aunty Mary laughed. "Not fish. Feis. Sounds like fresh. It means festival. A celebration of music and dance. Basically, it's a dance competition."

"What's she wearing?" asked Patrick staring at the photograph. "She looks like she's got her school uniform on but with ballet pumps."

"That's her dance costume," said Aunty Mary. "It was a bit like school uniform. We couldn't afford expensive outfits. I think her shoes are still up in the loft. We could go and have a look if you like?"

"Yes, please!" said Grace.

"Can I come too?" asked Patrick, who liked the idea of discovering hidden stuff.

"Of course. Family day out in the loft," Aunty Mary laughed.

"Count me out," said Dad. "I'm afraid of the dark."

Chapter 4

Ten minutes later, the children were sitting on the boarded floor of the loft surrounded by boxes, clothes and dust.

"It's been a while since anyone has been up here," apologised Aunty Mary.

"Cool!" shouted Patrick, who had found an old pair of football boots and was trying to put them on.

"Be careful. You don't know what you'll find inside. Might be a couple of spiders!"

Patrick promptly dropped them.

Grace was looking at some clothes hanging on a metal rail. At the end of the rail were about four or five colourful dresses with long sleeves. Most of them had patterns on the skirt and bodice, some had crosses and there were some funny looking hexagon shapes.

"These were the dresses we wore for Irish dancing," said Aunty Mary, blowing off dust that had settled on the shoulders and arms. "They must be twenty years old now."

"They're still beautiful though," said Grace, feeling the intricate lace pattern on one of the dresses.

"Now, where is that box I'm looking for?" said Aunty Mary, as she put the dress back on the rail.

Grace held a black and gold dress up to

her shoulders. It looked like it would fit her. She wondered if she should try it on.

"Found it!" shouted Aunty Mary. "I knew it was here somewhere."

Grace put the dress back and hurried over to her aunt who was crouched over a battered looking cardboard box.

Aunty Mary opened up the flap on the outside of the box and pulled out a pair of black ballet pumps. She gave them to Grace.

"These were your mum's dance shoes."

The black leather was worn around the toe area and the suede bottom was bare in places.

Long black laces were wrapped around the shoes to keep them together. Grace sat down and took off her trainers. Then she started to unravel the laces and gently and slowly pulled the black shoes on. Aunty Mary bent down and crossed the laces over and around the bottom of Grace's foot.

"They fit," shouted a delighted Grace. She began to point her toes and jump from one foot to the other.

"Careful!" cried Aunty Mary. "There isn't a lot of room up here. Why don't you go downstairs now and I'll be there in a minute."

Grace climbed down the loft stairs and went to find Dad.

"Dad, look at these. Look at me. I'm dancing." Grace proceeded to skip all around the room.

"Wow! Look at you. You're a natural," said her Dad.

"I don't know about that but it does feel wonderful."

"Then maybe we should find out about dance lessons when we get home? What do you

think?"

Grace's eyes widened with excitement. "Can we? That would be brilliant." She rushed to hug him.

Aunty Mary came into the room carrying

another battered cardboard box.

"I found these and thought you would like to see." She opened up the box to uncover piles of photographs. Grace held them up. There were lots of photos of her mum wearing her costumes and holding trophies.

"Wow! She must have been really good to win all of these."

Aunty Mary laughed. "Well, she did go to a lot of competitions."

"Dad has said he will take me to a dance class so I can learn properly," said an excited Grace.

"That's great but I was wondering if you would like to go to a class here so you can see what happens? I have a friend who runs the local dance class and I'm sure she wouldn't mind if you came along."

"Can I, Dad?" asked Grace.

"That would be great, Mary. Thank you,"

said Dad smiling appreciatively.

They looked at the photographs for the rest of the afternoon. It felt good to share something between them. Hearing Aunty Mary explain who was in each photo and what was happening made Grace feel like mum was still with them, just for a while.

After tea, Aunty Mary phoned her friend who ran the dance class.

"That's all sorted," said Aunty Mary, as she walked back into the kitchen. "You can join them tomorrow at the church hall at ten o'clock."

Grace hugged Aunty Mary so hard she almost squeezed all the air out of her. After she had finally stopped hugging, Grace announced she was off to bed.

"But it's only eight o'clock," said her Dad, looking at his watch confused.

"I need to go to bed now," explained

Grace. "Tomorrow can't come soon enough for me."

Chapter 5

The next morning Grace awoke to the smell of sausages and bacon wafting up the stairs.

"I thought you'd like a fry," said Aunty Mary, when she saw Grace standing in the doorway. "You'll need lots of energy if you're going to do some Irish dancing this morning."

Grace didn't think she'd be able to eat anything she was so excited but she sat to the table anyway. Patrick was already eating cereal. "What will I wear?"

"A t-shirt and leggings will be fine and you can take your mum's shoes as they seem to fit. Now, start with some cereal and eat up!"

ordered Aunty Mary.

***

At exactly ten o'clock, Grace and Aunty Mary stood outside the church hall door. Grace timidly pushed the door open and looked inside. There were some girls sitting on the stage and some on the floor all lacing up their dance shoes. More girls came in behind them and then Grace noticed there were a few boys too. Music began to blast out and then a loud voice shouted over the top. "Warm up! Off you go!"

The loud voice belonged to the dance teacher who came over to Aunty Mary and Grace.

"Mary! How lovely to see you. And you must be Grace. Nice to meet you." She put out her hand. Grace shook it. Her hand was warm like her smile, although the booming voice made Grace slightly nervous. "My name is Bridget. I just want you to have fun today, okay?"

Grace nodded.

"Amy, will you look after Grace today, please? Show her what to do?"

"Grace, I'll be here later when you've

finished," said Aunty Mary, as she walked out of the front door.

A petite, brown haired girl came over and beckoned for Grace to follow. They sat on the stage and Amy helped Grace lace up her shoes. Then they stood up to join in the warm up, running around the room on the count of one, jumping on the spot on two and ducking down on three. This was fun.

When the warm ups were finished, the girls stood on the wooden floor and waited for Bridget to speak.

"Okay, let's go through the Reel to begin with. Grace, come here and you can watch first of all. Then we will break it down for you."

Grace watched the children pointing their toes and then jumping and crossing their leg in front of their body, all the time skipping around the room in time to the music. When they were finished, Amy came over to Grace and talked her through the main step. "So with the right foot you jump on one, then the left foot lands in front and then the right foot goes behind to join the left foot on three. Then you repeat it all again."

Grace practised while Amy called out the steps.

"That's great. This is called the lead round and there are three steps to each dance. The first step is a cut, when one leg is bent and raised up across the other leg."

Amy demonstrated and Grace copied.

"The second step is a cross over, when one foot crosses in front and the other crosses behind. Like this." Again, Amy showed her what to do and Grace copied.

"And finally, the last step is jump, two, three, jump, two, three, walk back, walk back and jump, two, three."

"Got all that? I know it's a lot to learn so let's take it slowly."

Grace and Amy went over the steps again and again until Grace felt more confident. "You're keeping in time with the music beautifully," encouraged Amy.

"I keep forgetting to bring my leg up and go straight into the jumps."

"Don't worry! It takes a lot of practice. I've been doing this for ten years."

Suddenly Grace didn't feel so bad.

Chapter 6

When they were finished, Bridget put the music back on again and everyone took up their starting position, right foot pointing forwards. Bridget stood next to Grace and held her hand. "I'll guide you around the room. Five, six, seven, eight."

Grace went through the steps concentrating hard. She began with her right leg and then stepped forward with her left and all in time with the music. She jumped and skipped all around the room with Bridget calling out the steps to remind her. Grace didn't want the dance to end. She felt like she was flying, light and happy. When the music did finally finish Grace realised how out of breath she was, her cheeks and hands warm.

"Well done, Grace!" Bridget applauded. "You kept to the rhythm beautifully."

"I went wrong on some of the steps though and used the wrong foot to lead off with second time round."

Bridget looked at her sternly. "This was your first time dancing and I must say I was impressed. You may be a natural, although I don't want to say that too soon. Even so, you still have to practise and practise the steps over and over again to get it right. It takes time and dedication. If you can do that, you'll do well."

Bridget turned to face the rest of the class. "Let's go over the light jig next!"

The girls and boys split into age groups and one by one each group went over the light jig on the stage, while the others watched and had a quick drink from their water bottles. If someone in the group made a mistake, then the music was stopped and the whole of the group would start again from the beginning.

Grace had a go at some of the simple

steps but had to watch the older, more experienced dancers when it came to dancing in their 'heavy shoes' the girls called them. Grace thought they looked like tap shoes and they made a great noise when they stamped their feet.

When Aunty Mary went back to collect Grace later on, she found a red faced, beaming young girl. She looked so happy, like someone who had discovered the best secret in the world.

"I can see you enjoyed that," said Aunty Mary, as Grace raced towards her and squeezed her round the waist.

"That was the best thing I have ever done. It's really tiring and you have to concentrate so hard but it feels amazing when you get the steps right."

Just then Bridget came over. "You're right, Mary. She loves it and I think she may be very good, if she puts the practice in."

"I will, I promise," replied Grace.

"I can recommend some good clubs in London if Grace is interested in continuing," said Bridget.

Both Grace and Aunty Mary nodded.

"Thank you, Bridget and thank you, Amy, for helping me with the steps."

The girls waved at Grace and smiled.

"Anytime you are visiting, you pop in and see us, okay?" said Bridget as she hugged Grace goodbye.

Grace began to hurry out of the door and down the street.

"What's the rush?" asked Aunty Mary, struggling to keep up with her. "I thought you liked Irish dancing."

"I do," Grace shouted back. "It's just I need to show Dad what I've learnt and I need to practise!"

Chapter 7

For the next two days, everyone heard Grace practising. When she was upstairs, the floorboards creaked as she hopped left, right, left and then right, left, right around the bedroom floor. When she was downstairs she would call out the steps as she was dancing them.

"Cut, forward, hop back, hop...No, that's wrong. It's hop back, two, three, four and forward jump. No, no, that's not right!"

"Who are you talking to?" said her Dad, as he peered around the kitchen door to see what was going on.

"Oh, no-one. I have to go through the steps or I'll forget."

"I said I'll take you to a dance class when we go home," said her dad.

"I know. I just don't want to forget."

"Grace, don't be so silly. You've just started learning. Everyone forgets to begin with."

"Not me! I want to practise until I get it right. I want to be perfect. I want to be as good as mum was."

Grace's eyes started to fill with tears. Her dad hugged her until the tears stopped.

"She was so proud of you and would have been if you were Irish dancing or not. She used to call you our very own amazing Grace!"

"What's the matter?" asked Patrick, walking into the kitchen.

"Nothing," Grace replied, pushing herself away from her dad. "Just having a hug. Do you want me to show you this step?"

Patrick pulled a face like he'd just smelt something nasty. "No! Dancing's for girls!"

"Actually, it isn't. Boys do Irish dancing

too. Some of them are amazing!"

"Well, I don't want to. All you ever do is dance or talk about it? Do you want to come and play football?"

Grace suddenly felt sorry for her twin brother. She hadn't spent much time with him recently and he was right. She was always dancing.

"Okay," she agreed and they ran outside.

***

"Score!" shouted Patrick, with his arms in the air raised in victory.

"Well, you do spend most of your time playing football. You should be good at it," said Grace, picking the football out of the goal net for the tenth time that afternoon.

Just then Aunty Mary shouted up the garden. "Grace! I have news for you."

Grace looked at Patrick and they both ran up to Aunty Mary.

"Bridget has just phoned me. She said they are putting on a pre Christmas dance show tomorrow and she was so impressed by you the

other day she wondered if you'd like to join in?"

Grace's eyes were nearly as wide as her smile. "I'd love to!"

"They are having another practice tonight at five o'clock so I'll take you over later."

Grace hugged Aunty Mary. This was turning out to be the best holiday ever.

Chapter 8

The next morning Grace woke bleary eyed and very tired. Even though she was exhausted from all the dancing she had done the day before, she was so excited she couldn't sleep.

She kept running through all the steps in her head. 'Right and right, and left and left and forward, hop back and right and right. Or was it left and left and right and right, cut back, hop forward and left and left.'

It had all started to jumble up in her head and then she had had some weird dreams. In one dream she was being chased down the street by a giant pair of dance shoes that were trying to tread on her. None of it made any sense.

"It's just your brain processing all the information you gave it yesterday," said Aunty Mary, after Grace had described her dream.

Grace was trying really hard to eat the bacon and sausage Aunty Mary had made for breakfast but she was too nervous. Her stomach was full already with butterflies.

"Only a few more hours to go," said her dad, eating the unwanted food off her plate.

A few hours later, Grace was busy practising her short dance routine. She had loved being part of a group and skipping round the room with everyone else. She was dancing the Reel. Normally, the first dance you learnt. Bridget had choreographed a routine with the older girls showing off their more advanced skills and the younger girls and Grace slotted in between. The older girls had been so nice to Grace. Encouraging her when she went wrong and praising her when she got it right. She hoped she wouldn't let them down. She would find out tonight.

***

Later in the day, Aunty Mary and Grace set off for the dance show. It was being held in the local church hall in the centre of town so they didn't have far to go.

"Right. Are you okay?" Do you have everything you need? Are you okay?" repeated Aunty Mary as they arrived at the hall. Suddenly Aunty Mary seemed more nervous than Grace.

"I'm okay. I promise. Don't worry about me."

"Right, well, break a leg, as they say... I think they say that. Oh dear, maybe they say something else for Irish dance shows." Aunty Mary wrinkled her forehead and looked more concerned than ever.

Grace hugged her. "I'm fine, honestly. I couldn't have done this without you. Now I must go. I don't want to be late for my first show." And with that she hurried inside.

***

It was pandemonium in the hall. There

were people everywhere. Some were putting out chairs, some were carrying tables and some were up ladders fiddling with the lights. There were women in another room taking cups and saucers out of boxes and laying plates on top of the worktop.

It was a hive of activity but Grace couldn't see any of the girls.

"They're in the back," said one of the

women, pointing to where they were, when she noticed Grace standing there looking lost.

Grace walked around the back of the stage and into a cloud of hairspray. She coughed to clear her throat and took in the scene before her eyes. A few of the girls were sitting down while others were busy hovering over them, backcombing their hair and spraying streams of hairspray.

"My turn," shouted one of the girls as they swapped over and the fully coiffured girl became the hairdresser. Some of the older ladies were standing over them, pins in their mouths, which they removed one by one and placed securely in the girls' hair.

"Dancers!" shouted Bridget over the noise. "We need one final practice and then you can finish off getting ready. I want you on the stage now, please!"

Grace found a small space in the corner of

the room and put her bag down. She took out her mum's shoes, laced them up and took her place on the stage.

Chapter 9

An hour later they were back in the changing room and soon the room was filled with hairspray and bursts of glitter falling slowly to the floor. The older girls were now applying some brown stuff to their legs.

"What are they doing?" Grace asked Siobhan, who was her partner in the dance.

"Fake tan. So their legs are nice and

brown next to their white socks. Makes their legs stand out."

"Do we have to do that?" asked Grace slightly horrified by the thought. She hated applying sun tan lotion which didn't look as bad as this.

"No. Lots of the girls like to do it as their legs are so white you can't see the difference where the legs finish and the socks start. Don't worry. You're wearing tights," said Siobhan laughing. "Come on. I must get my hair done."

Siobhan sat down and one of the mums began to brush her long, wavy blonde hair into a high ponytail on her head. Then she skilfully twisted the hair to form a bun and pinned it in place. Finally she pulled the bun through a small circular sponge. Grace found out it was called a doughnut! 'It's all about food,' thought Grace. 'Bun and doughnut. Is there an éclair too?' she wondered.

"What's that?" said Grace, when she saw the mum pick up what looked like a small animal and began to put it on Siobhan's head.

"It's a wig," laughed Siobhan, seeing Grace's screwed up face. "Don't worry. You get used to them. If we didn't wear them our heads would look tiny in a our wide, elaborate dresses and anyway, it's fun to dress up!"

"Now, it's your turn." Grace swapped seats with Siobhan and the same mum began to brush her hair. "No wig for you today but we will curl your hair and make it pretty," said the mum, smiling at Grace.

Ten minutes later and Grace was ready for part two.

"Make up next!" Siobhan led Grace over to another group of mums who were busy applying foundation and lipstick. "We normally wear make up for shows. Bridget likes us to wear it. The stage lights can make you look ill and washed out if you don't."

Grace let one of the mums rub a light brown liquid onto her face followed by some pink blusher and a lip-gloss. When it was done Grace stared at herself in the mirror. She looked older. It felt weird but as Siobhan said it was only for the show.

"Okay, everyone! We have thirty minutes until the show starts. Warm-ups please!" shouted Bridget over the noise of chattering, spraying and dancing feet.

***

At exactly seven o'clock the girls took up their positions on the stage. They were hidden from the audience by a red velvet curtain. Grace was at the side of the stage nervously waiting. She wasn't going on for a while but Bridget told her she could watch from there until it was time to join the others.

Grace could hear the audience talking on

the other side of the curtain. She knew Aunty
Mary, her dad and Patrick would be there

somewhere in the crowd, looking on proudly.

Suddenly the audience stopped talking
and Bridget's voice sang out loudly on the
microphone.

"Thank you all so much for coming here

tonight. The girls and boys have worked really hard to produce this show and we hope you enjoy it."

As the audience cheered, music blared out from the speakers and the curtains began to rise. The dancers stood still like statues in the darkness. Then all of a sudden the spotlights shone down on them and the music began its gentle rhythm. They danced their céili routine. Dancing in and out of each other, dancing in a line, in pairs, in fours and smiling the whole time. Grace thought they were amazing.

At the end of the routine the crowd cheered and clapped and Bridget went back onto the stage to introduce the next part of the show.

Grace heard Bridget explain that the next dance was to be danced by Kirsty, an older girl who was very experienced. This dance was her set piece for the World Championships in April.

Kirsty danced across the whole of the

stage. Grace had never seen someone jump so high or stand up on the toes of her shoes. She jumped and kicked and glided in perfect rhythm with the music.

The crowd whooped and cheered when Kirsty finished her dance. 'These dancers are so good,' Grace thought to herself and then felt a little foolish for thinking she could be half as good as them. There was no time to think about this as she needed to go and get her dress on.

Five minutes later she was ready. Grace felt like a princess. She was wearing a soft purple costume with a white satin skirt. All across the neck and down to the skirt were hundreds of crystals and when the lights caught them they sparkled all the colours of the rainbow.

"Thank you, ladies and gentlemen," bellowed out Bridget's voice over the microphone. "I can tell you enjoyed that. For our next dance we have choreographed it using all the children from the dance school including a special visitor from London. Please could you give them all a big hand!"

And with that the crowd cheered loudly again. Grace was suddenly very nervous.

"Places, please," said one of the older girls and the dancers stood in their positions on stage ready for the start of the dance. Grace stood at the side of the stage next to the curtains.

She breathed deeply to help with her nerves and waited for the moment she would join the rest of the dancers.

The music began and off they went. The older ones danced in a line, their feet tapping the beat the whole time. Then they split into smaller groups, kicking and jumping quickly across the stage.

Bridget came up behind Grace who was almost hanging onto the curtain she wanted to see the dancing so much. "I'll let you know when you go on. Just like we practised, okay?"

Grace nodded but kept her eyes on the stage and the dancers. Before Bridget could gently push her on, Grace had gone skipping left and left and right and right all around the older dancers on the stage. She moved in between the groups like a coloured thread weaving through material.

Finally, she joined a younger group of

dancers in the centre of the stage where they stood still waiting for the older ones to finish their part. On command they all moved together, stamping left then right, hopping forward and back. They all did a sliding step with their left foot, and then their right foot and finally raised their arms and joined hands with the dancer next to them.

The music stopped and all Grace could

hear was the sound of whooping and cheering and clapping in time with the fast beating of her heart.

The dancers bowed once, then twice. The cheering continued so they bowed again. Grace peered into the audience and saw Aunty Mary, Patrick and Dad on their feet clapping and waving at her.

This was a moment she would never forget and everyone who saw the smile on Grace's face that night knew it too.

Chapter 10

The next morning at breakfast, Grace was very quiet and Dad was concerned. The last few days he'd never seen her so happy but now her face looked like it did the first morning they'd arrived.

"Cheer up, Grace! You look so miserable and you've had a brilliant time here, haven't you?"

"Oh, yes Dad, I know. It's been amazing but..."

Grace couldn't finish her sentence and Dad knew why.

"We have to go home sometime."

"I know. It's just I will miss the dancing and I'll miss Aunty Mary and..." Grace's eyes started to water and she swallowed hard so she didn't start crying.

Just then Aunty Mary walked into the

room. "Grace, could I have a word, please?" Grace followed her into the hallway.

"Do you remember looking at this photograph when you first got here?" She was pointing to the one of her mum wearing her dance costume and shoes. Grace nodded.

"A lot has happened since that day but I need you to know that you are taking two very important things away with you."

"What's that?"

"The first thing is Irish Dancing. I don't know why but it's like it was meant to be, you seeing the photograph, then seeing the girls dance in the festival and then Bridget saying you could join in a class. Dancing is in your blood. Your mum loved it and so do you. And you can do Irish dancing wherever you are."

"And what's the second thing?" asked Grace.

"Me!"

Grace looked at Aunty Mary with a confused expression on her face. "How can I take you with me? You can't get in my suitcase."

"I haven't been able to help you until now but I want you to know that if you need anything, anything at all or want to talk about your mum or anything really, then all you have to do is wish it and I'll be there."

"Like a fairy godmother," said Grace, her

eyes all sparkling and excited.

"Yes, just like a fairy godmother, except I don't do actual wishes! I'm a fairy godmother with technology. You can phone, email me, Skype and FaceTime me too, all at the click of a button and I'll be there. And I promise to visit, if you will too?"

"You really are my fairy godmother," said Grace, hugging Aunty Mary round the waist. "You helped to turn me into a princess for the day when I was dancing and more importantly, you have given me the chance to do something special, something that makes me happy."

Grace squeezed her tightly and Aunty Mary's tears slowly rolled down her face.

"You phone me as soon as you arrive home and we will look at some of the dance schools Bridget recommended, okay? This isn't the end Grace. This is the beginning of a new adventure for you and I know you're going to love it."

"Come on you two," shouted Dad from outside. "I can't pack the car by myself."

***

Half an hour later Grace, Dad, Patrick and Aunty Mary all stared at the car. It looked like an over stuffed teddy bear

"Why is it you seem to leave with more stuff than you brought in the first place?" said her dad, laughing at the mountain of suitcases and extra bags that had now been acquired.

They were definitely leaving with more. There were her mum's dance shoes and one of her dresses but they were leaving with much more than stuff.

Grace now had many more memories of her mum. She had started a new adventure with Irish dancing and she couldn't wait to see where it would take her.

***

Find out what happens to Grace in the next story in the series 'The Light Jig'- coming soon.

About Amanda Miles

Amanda Miles taught primary school children for many years before deciding to publish her books. A long time ago, she had two Irish dance lessons and then gave up.

Her daughter, Grace, began Irish dancing at the age of five and loved it. She was the inspiration behind this story and the introduction to the amazing world of Irish Dancing.

As well as writing children's books, Amanda Miles is the Chair of Governors at a primary school, wife, mother of twins and general peacekeeper. She lives in London.

For more information about her books go to www.wordsmom.com

CELL WARS

ISBN: 1494292491

By Amanda Miles

Bands is just like any young soldier. He keeps watch, defends against his enemies and risks his life to save others. It's the job he was born to do. The duty of a white blood cell.

Join Bands in his mission to protect the human body from deadly bacteria and find out how a bruise and scab are made. A fictional science book for all children.

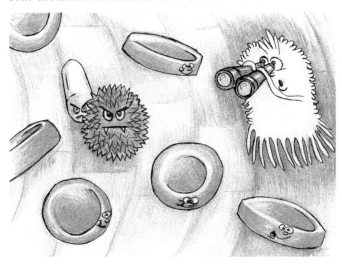

"A fantastic book for kids. The author cleverly balances adventure and biology. Highly recommended and a SILVER MEDAL WINNER!" *Wishing Shelf Awards 2015*

"An ingenious idea that teaches children about the blood system, delightfully illustrated." *The Rubery Book Awards 2014.*

"A Great Way to Learn about How Our Bodies Work" *K. A. Wheatley TOP 500 REVIEWERVINE VOICE MARCH 2014*

CELL WARS ll

ISBN: 150318661X

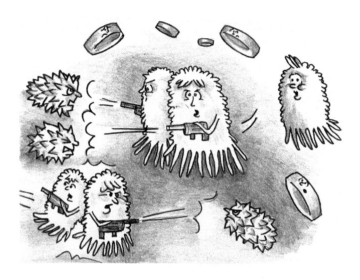

By Amanda Miles

Bands, a white blood cell, is on a dangerous mission to find and destroy all the deadly flu viruses rapidly spreading through the body. His teacher, Master Baso and Captain Neutro have taught him so much but will it be enough?

Follow the adventures of Bands in the second book of the award winning 'Cell Wars' series and find out if it is the flu virus or Bands who is exterminated?

CPSIA information can be obtained
at www.ICGtesting.com
Printed in the USA
BVHW041859021218
534587BV00019B/419/P